Bottersnikes

S. A. Wakefield lives with his wife on a small farm, about fifty miles north of Sydney. He loves the Australian bush and his feelings for it, coupled with a wonderful sense of fun and fantasy, bubble forth in the hilarious adventures of the scaly Bottersnikes and the squashy Gumbles.

Desmond Digby's beautifully witty illustrations mirror the imaginative quality of Sam Wakefield's text. Like the author, Desmond Digby has a great affection for the Australian landscape. Born in New Zealand, he has a high reputation as a stage designer and satiric painter. His drawings are beautifully executed, with an eye for the small details in which children delight.

S. A. Wakefield

Bottersnikes and Gumbles

Illustrated by

Desmond Digby

Piper Books

For Susan, Michael and Aleta

First published 1967 by William Collins Pty Ltd, Sydney
Piccolo edition published 1984 by Pan Books Ltd
This Piper edition published 1988 by Pan Books Ltd,
Cavaye Place, London SW10 9PG
Text © S. A. Wakefield 1967
Illustrations © Desmond Digby 1967
ISBN 0 330 28191 7
9 8 7 6 5 4
Phototypeset by Input Typesetting Ltd, London
Printed and bound in Great Britain by
Cox & Wyman Ltd, Reading

CONTENTS

CHAPTER ONE

Running Down to the Beach

Bottersnikes are the laziest creatures, probably, in the whole world.

They are too lazy to dig burrows, like rabbits, or to find hollow trees to live in as the small animals do, and would be horrified at the work of building nests, like birds. Bottersnikes find their homes readymade, in rubbish heaps. When they find a pile of tins, pots, pans and junk, they think it is lovely, and crawl in. And live there, sleeping mostly. Best of all they like the rubbish heaps along dusty roadsides in the lonely Australian bush, where they can sleep for weeks, undisturbed.

Once, in a rubbish heap like this, two long black ears poked out of a watering can. The ears came first because they were twice as long as the head they belonged to. Between the ears appeared an ugly green face with slanted eyes, a nose like a cheese grater and a mean mouth with pointed teeth sticking out. The skin was wrinkly all over and little toadstools grew where the eyebrows should have been.

This was the King of the Bottersnikes. He squeezed out of the watering can.

The King's ears turned bright red because he was angry — this always happens with Bottersnikes when they get angry — and the cause of his temper was a thistle growing through the bottom of his bed. But he was too lazy to pull it out and just stood there looking, with his ears growing redder. Near him he saw an old rusting car, propped against a gum tree. What a palace that would make for a Bottersnike King! 'If someone would open the door,' he thought, 'I would get in.'

8

So the King yelled at the top of his voice for help — and very loud that is; but the other Bottersnikes, all twenty or so of the King's band, snored loudly from their beds in the rubbish to show they had not heard.

This meant that the King would have to pull someone out of bed, kick him and twist his tail till he woke up, and make him open the car door, so that the King could get in. Bottersnikes go to no end of trouble to do things the easiest way. 'There is no one, no one at all,' the King growled, 'who will help.' His ears glowed in a royal rage that was quite terrible to see.

As the King was yelling for help the Gumbles happened to be passing, which was just their bad luck. They were on their way down the hill to a little stream they knew of, called Earlyfruit Creek, where the water flowed into quiet pools and banks of sand made tiny beaches just right for Gumble paddling.

'Hey, you!' bawled the King to the Gumbles, 'Come and open this door and help me in.'

The Gumbles were a bit astonished, as all their friends in the Bush were much politer than this, but being cheerful little creatures and always ready to lend a hand, like good Brownies, they said: 'Well, all right, if it won't take too long, because we're in a hurry to get to the creek, you see.'

'Don't argue,' the King said. 'Just do as you're told.'

By climbing up each other's backs the Gumbles managed to open the car door, and with a one-two-three altogether *shove* they heaved the King into his new palace. Hearing the strange voices, the other Bottersnikes decided to wake up. They peered at these funny little creatures they'd not seen before and asked: 'What are these?'

'Useful,' the King said, clambering on to the steering wheel, 'That's what they are. Grab 'em.'

'Here, just a minute — you can't do that,' the Gumbles

cried, all speaking at once, 'We only stopped to lend a hand. We're just running down to the beach. For a paddle in the cool water.'

'Got you!' shouted the Bottersnikes, and they grabbed those little Gumbles — this was quite easy, for though they are so lazy Bottersnikes can move faster than Gumbles when they have to because their legs are longer. And when they grabbed them they discovered a peculiar thing about Gumbles. They discovered that you can squeeze Gumbles to any shape you like without hurting them, and that if you press them very hard they flatten out like pancakes and cannot pop back to their proper shapes unless helped.

'This,' said the King, watching, 'Is more useful than ever.'

The Bottersnikes blinked. They couldn't see why it was useful at all — silly, squashy things, they thought.

'Because,' the King growled, 'We can pop 'em into something and squash 'em down hard so's they can't get away, and when I want some more work done they'll be ready and waiting to do it.'

Now the Bottersnikes began to get the idea. They would have servants for ever, to tidy up and keep them comfortable. 'Hoo, hoo!' they yelled, 'What'll we pop 'em into?'

'Jam tins,' roared the King. Another good idea! Naturally there were hundreds of them lying in the rubbish. 'The proper thing is to shout "Got you!" and grab 'em, and pop 'em into jam tins.'

'What a rotten thing to think of,' cried the Gumbles, 'When we only stopped to —'

'Got you!' shouted the Bottersnikes, and they grabbed the Gumbles and popped them into jam tins. And squashed them down hard, with horny fists. There were more than enough Gumbles for each Bottersnike to grab one. Some of the fattest, in fact, grabbed two.

How they snuffled through their noses — which meant that they were laughing — how they rorted and snorted and hooed

with glee at what they had done. 'We done ourselves a good turn,' the King announced, 'We done a good day's work.'

Exhausted at the thought of this, they fell asleep at once, and the tinned Gumbles were left in the hot sun all afternoon, thinking of the cool creek where they had meant to paddle. Now, it seemed, they would never go there again.

Towards evening some of the Bottersnikes woke up, disturbed by snores from the King's palace — most royal ones, like trombones blaring. 'All very well for 'im,' the Bottersnikes thought, their ears going red, 'But we ain't got palaces to sleep in, and we ain't comfy, and what's to be done?' Then they remembered the Gumbles. 'Stop being lazy in them tins,' they ordered, 'And come and put our places comfy.'

So the Gumbles were hauled out of the tins and put to work building bigger and better rubbish heaps for the Bottersnikes to crawl into; a nastier job for Gumbles would be impossible to find. 'Harder, harder,' the Bottersnikes bawled, 'And don't try and run away, 'cos we're watching you!'

But they did not see one little Gumble under the King's car, where he was puzzling over a tin-opener he had found. This Gumble was the one who had Tinks — every Tink was a good idea — and as soon as he discovered how the tin-opener worked a real beauty came to him: *Tink!* Clear as if you had tapped the edge of a glass with a spoon.

Up jumped Tinkingumble with his bright idea and peered cautiously from behind a wheel. 'Pssst! Bring me the jam tins one by one,' he whispered to Happigumble and Merrigumble nearby. 'Mind they don't see you!'

While the Bottersnikes were trying the new heaps to see if they were comfy, and squabbling over who should have the comfiest, they rolled the jam tins under the car where Tinkingumble cut the bottoms out of every one, working fast and secretly; then Happigumble and Merrigumble rolled them

back again taking care to keep the parts together so that they looked all right from the top. The job was done just in time.

'It ain't good,' the Bottersnikes growled, 'Not a bit good, but it'll have to do for tonight 'cos we're tired, and you'll have to work harder tomorrow.' They shouted 'Got you!' and grabbed the Gumbles and popped them into the jam tins, and snuffled their noses about it because they knew they'd have servants tomorrow and forever. Then they went to sleep.

When they were snoring safely Tinkingumble called 'Now!' and the Gumbles tried to stand up. The cut-out bottoms of the tins fell away nicely, just as planned, but they were still stuck in the round parts — absolutely wodged in.

'How are we going to get away?' said Happigumble. 'My legs are so squashed up I can hardly move!'

'I hadn't thought of that,' Tinkingumble said unhappily. A Tink came to the rescue as he spoke — only a small one, but quite clear. Following Tinkingumble's, the jam tins blundered towards the road banging into each other as they went — it nearly made them giggly, and Gumbles are quite hopeless when they go giggly — and there they rocked themselves until the tins fell over on their sides, and the slope of the hill did the rest. The Gumbles ran down to the beach in their jam tins much, much faster than any Bottersnike could have chased them.

An Owl, who saw all the tins rolling down the hill in the moonlight, was so surprised that he flew straight into a moult, and declared he'd never seen such a sight in all his years of hooting.

At the bottom of the hill the Gumbles shot off the road into the Bush, where a friendly bandicoot poked them out of the tins with his long nose. They put the jam tins in a bin marked Please Be Tidy and spent the rest of the night paddling at their favourite beach, for Gumbles are too busy having fun to waste time sleeping and there is no one to tell them when to go to bed.

CHAPTER TWO

Willigumble — Late as Usual

'We'll never let ourselves get caught by those creatures again,' the Gumbles said, next morning. 'Never, never, never, never!'

'We'll go away where they'll never find us,' Happigumble said. 'One more paddle first, though.'

Someone suddenly cried, as they were paddling: 'Where's Willigumble? He's not here!'

They called for him but there was no answer, and searched up and down the creek bank but there was no sign; and after much anxious hunting they sat down and looked at each other glumly. No one said a word, but in each Gumblehead was the dreadful thought: *Willigumble must have been left behind with the Bottersnikes.* Little Willi, on his own. He was the smallest Gumble of them all.

Happigumble jumped up. 'We'll have to go and rescue him,' he said, 'Somehow.'

They started up the hill towards the rubbish heaps. Somehow they would get him back.

They had not gone far before a coloured thing came hurtling down the hill towards them. Faster and faster it came, off the road it bounced, sending them scattering, and lodged against a bush. It was an asparagus tin, with something inside that looked like a lump of dough — but when they pulled it out and squeezed it into shape, it was Willigumble. He was giggling all over.

'Fatso of a Bottersnike couldn't read,' Willigumble gurgled, 'Put me in the wrong tin!'

'Silly old Willi, late as usual,' the Gumbles joked. But there was great relief.

'The Bottersnikes did kick up a rumpus when they found you'd all gone,' Willigumble told them. 'They turned the rubbish heaps upside down and all they found was the bottom of the jam tins; and then Owl told them about the tins rolling down the hill in the moonlight — disgusting, he called it, 'cos it scared the game — and the Bottersnikes told Owl not to be an idiot, it couldn't happen, they said, and Owl told the Bottersnikes it could and did, and there was a fearful argument; and then the Bottersnikes said: "We'll try it then, just to show what a fool Owl is," and they took my tin across to the road and gave it a push — and here I am!'

'And there are the Bottersnikes coming after us,' cried Happigumble, 'And O, grasshoppers, look at their ears! What are we going to do? Tinkingumble, have a Tink quickly!'

Two or three of them squeezed Tinkingumble till he was nearly all head, because he had his best Tinks that way; and meanwhile the Bottersnikes were waddling down the hill shouting furiously and blaming Owl for letting their last Gum-

ble get away. Their ears were brilliant. In their horny hands they carried new jam tins.

The Tink came in a moment, clear as a cricket's chirrup, and the Gumbles crowded round. 'What is it, Tinkingumble? What's the Tink?'

'We must cross the creek,' he said.

'Yes, yes, but how? It's too deep!' For Gumbles, though they love to splash in shallow water, cannot swim.

'In Willigumble's tin, of course,' he said. So they took Willigumble's asparagus tin, the only one that didn't have its bottom cut out, and using gum leaves as oars they paddled over in loads of four or five, with one oarsman bringing the tin back for the next trip.

The Bottersnikes arrived at the sandy beach just as the last tinful rowed away — and there they stopped. Bottersnikes hate water. If they get wet, they shrink, and have to be hung up to dry. So they stood on the bank and raged. Safe on the other side the Gumbles pulled rude faces, cheekily waved goodbye and scuttled into the Bush.

The long ears glowed red hot with fury as the Bottersnikes howled and growled on the creek bank, until at last the King roared 'Snonk!' and they became quieter.

The King said: 'We will make a Gumbletrap.'

'A trap to catch Gumbles in — oh, clever, clever!' the Bottersnikes shouted. But what did a Gumbletrap look like? The King knew, perhaps, but he wouldn't tell them, he just stood there tickling his stomach with the end of his tail.

A Bottersnike called Glob spoke up. 'Suppose there was a hole in the ground and we covered it with branches so's they couldn't see it, then when they walked over it they'd all fall in.'

The King thought about this for two minutes and said: 'Just what I was going to say myself. Dig the hole.'

This looked too much like work, so Glob said, a bit nervously: 'Why don't we get Smiggles to dream one?'

For very lazy people dreaming can be a way of getting things done, and this Bottersnike named Smiggles was useful sometimes because whatever he dreamed of became real — until he went to sleep again, then his first dream vanished to make room for his next. The trouble was that no one knew whether Smiggles would dream what he was told to dream about or something quite different.

'Go to sleep, Smiggles,' the King ordered, 'And dream a hole. A big one.'

Smiggles went to sleep with no difficulty at all, and while they waited for the dream to come along the others pottered about looking for a bit of rubbish to make them feel at home. Presently two of these pottering Bottersnikes found an old weedy hole near the road that someone had dug ages ago, but they didn't know this; they said: 'Idiot, he's dreamed it in the wrong place,' and went and told the King.

'Move it,' the King said, 'Put it down by the creek.'

Four Bottersnikes picked the hole up by the corners and staggered with it to the creek bank, where they laid twigs and leaves over it so that it couldn't be seen from the top. Also they threw a dead branch across the creek to make a bridge, and the hole was just by the end of the bridge so that as the Gumbles stepped off they would be sure to fall in.

'A very cunning Gumbletrap,' they boasted — and then Smiggles woke up. 'Not a bad hole, Smig,' they told him, 'Except it was in the wrong place.'

'But I didn't dream a hole,' said Smiggles, puzzled. 'I dreamed a radiogram.' Which now stood awkwardly in the Bush — an expensive model, with lots of knobs and polished wood, though under the circumstances, not much use.

The King looked at Smiggles' dreamwork and snorted, then at the cunning Gumbletrap, but was not pleased with

that either. 'The Gumbles are too light,' he growled. 'They'll walk over the twigs without falling in. The idiot what thought of this Gumbletrap ought to have his head sat on.'

Glob hurriedly suggested that they should all get into the hole — for they had to hide somewhere — and pull the Gumbles down as they came across. The Bottersnikes liked the idea of this. They squeezed in the hole together, covered up again with leaves and twigs, snuffled their noses loudly and had a bit of a sleep while they waited.

All this time the Gumbles had been playing with some frogs farther down the creek. When the sun began to get hot they came back for another paddle at their favourite beach — all except Willigumble, who had stopped to tell some young tadpoles that they couldn't possibly play leapfrog until they had grown legs. The Gumbles were ever so cautious. On the far bank they stopped, looked and listened, wary for the merest whiff of danger; but no Bottersnikes could be seen; so they trotted over the bridge . . . and stepped carefully over the Gumbletrap, which failed to catch a single Gumble.

Gumbles are not so silly as to go crashing into covered holes — unless they go giggly, then they are silly enough for anything.

'Funny about that hole covered with leaves. I'm sure it wasn't there before,' Happigumble remarked, and because it is difficult not to look into a hole, to see how deep it is, they moved the leaves and peeped in.

It was a most extraordinary sight. Water from the creek had seeped into the hole while the Bottersnikes were dozing, and the great, fat creatures who had squeezed to get in had shrunk to the merest of red-eared blobs — no bigger than

Gumbles, in fact; and they were howling and clamouring to be let out, but naturally their voices had shrunk too.

The Gumbles went quite hopeless with giggling, at the sight.

'Get us out of here!' the Bottersnikes yelled in their ridiculous voices. 'Can't you see we're drowning?'

Shakily, the Gumbles lowered branches, and helped them out. Face to face with the shrunk 'snikes they burst into giggles all over again. 'You don't look nearly as bad this size,' they sniggered. 'It's a very good size to be, don't you think?'

Unfortunately, Bottersnikes are objectionable whatever their size. They were not in the least grateful. All they said was: 'If it hadn't been for you Gumbles we'd never have got in that hole in the first place,' and they found that although they were too small to grab the Gumbles properly they could pick the jam tins up and throw them over the Gumbles, making prisoners of them; this they did, shouting 'Got You!' as usual, and then they sat hard on the tins and waited for the wind to dry them out, so that they would grow again.

That was how things were when Willigumble came along.

'O, grasshoppers!' said Willi. Now he would have to do the rescuing, on his own.

'I wish I could have Tinks,' he said. But Tinkingumble was the only Tinker.

24

The Bottersnikes thought they may as well make some noise while they were growing up, and they shouted at the radio to play a tune. No one was big enough to reach the knob to switch it on, however, and the King growled, in what was supposed to be his deepest woof but was really only a tweet: 'Just like that idiot Smiggles. He don't dream right and what he do dream don't work.'

That gave Willigumble his big idea, though it did not come with a Tink. He nipped over the bridge and, keeping out of sight, crept to the back of the radio. A moment later a piping, squeaky voice came out of it: 'Hem! Exercises for small people, to make them bigger! are you ready, everyone?'

'Just what we want!' said Smiggles, very pleased with his radio and himself.

The radio made them wriggle and bend, waggle their ears and tie knots in their tails, but the Bottersnikes did all their growing exercises sitting down and just would not get off the jam tins.

At last the radio said: 'Now, you'll have grown an inch! Stand up, everyone, and try to touch the sky with the tops of your heads, and see how much you've grown.'

This the Bottersnikes could not resist doing. As they stood up to see how much they'd grown the jam tins behind them tipped over and the prisoner Gumbles escaped silently to the Bush.

'Close you eyes, everyone!' the radio said hurriedly, 'And listen carefully. Here's a brand new exercise that will make you grow two inches. Sit on the ground with your tails between your legs. Now put your feet behind your ears. Roll forward slowly until you can pick up the ends of your tails in your teeth —'

The Bottersnikes tried to do this complicated growing exercise and scorched their feet severely on their red hot ears. The radio gave a snort and a giggle then, and went off the air for good. Little Willigumble crawled out from the valves and things and — late as usual — rushed off to find his friends.

CHAPTER THREE

The Adventures of Chank

There was a fat, important Bottersnike called Chank. He was one of those who usually had two Gumbles to tidy up and keep him comfortable — that is, when the Bottersnikes *had* the Gumbles; but at the time that Chank began his adventures they had no Gumbles at all, not even Willi. Every morning they looked hopefully in their jam tins but the Gumbles were never there. They wanted the Gumbles back very badly because the middles of their scaly backs were all itchy and their wiry tails needed brushing. Their ears were red nearly all the time.

This Bottersnike named Chank liked to think that he was very brave and clever. His secret dream was that he should be the King of the Bottersnikes because he knew he was braver, and was sure he had more brains, than the real King.

One of the clever things he had done was to find an old straw hat amongst the rubbish. He called it his roof, and he wore it when it rained with his ears sticking out of two holes at the top. When it rained the other Bottersnikes had to crawl under their pots and pans and things (the King would get in his car) and stay there until it stopped, or they would shrink; but Chank would put his roof on and waddle about if he wanted to. It didn't matter about his ears sticking out. A Bottersnike is always angry when it rains and his ears get so hot the rain just sizzles off them.

Chank was very proud of his roof. He boasted like anything about it and would put it on whether it was raining or not, just to show off. He decided to put it on today to remind the others how clever he was. It wasn't raining but it was very windy; the gusts of wind were blowing loose paper about the rubbish heaps and rushing through the branches of the trees like giants in a hurry, and as Chank lifted his roof over his head the wind caught it and blew it clean away. It sailed away on the rush of the wind, over the rubbish heaps, and away to the Bush.

'Aow!' screamed Chank, 'My roof! My beautiful roof!'

The other Bottersnikes made their nose noises, which meant that they were laughing.

'It ain't funny!' Chank raged. 'It'll have to be brought back this instant.' He looked in his jam tins to see if his Gumbles were there, and they weren't, so he kicked the jam tins savagely and hurt his toe.

'Hey, Glob! Snorg! Be good 'snikes and go and find it for me,' he said. 'I'd go myself only I've hurt my toe.'

'All right,' said Glob, but he didn't move from the carpet sweeper he was sitting on.

'Go on, then,' shouted Chank.

'I have found it,' Glob said, 'It's stuck in that tree, about ten miles away.' They looked where he was pointing and could just see it caught in the branches of a big white gum; it wasn't ten miles really but it looked as far as that to a fat Bottersnike with short legs.

'Now all you've got to do,' said Snorg, 'Is to go and get it. Ain't you pleased?'

'Or you could wait till the wind changed and blew it back,' said Glob helpfully.

'What'll I do if it rains?' wailed Chank.

'Never mind, Chank. We'll lend you a jam tin,' they said, and snuffled their noses loudly.

This was to much! Very red in the ears, Chank shouted: 'Who'd want you to help anyway? You two ain't got enough brains to fill a peashooter — nincompoop Bottersnikes, that's what you are!'

He grabbed his favourite jam tin which had a wire handle to make it easier to carry (that was another of his clever ideas) and climbed over the rubbish. He was not keen about leaving on his own, but reminding himself he was a very brave and clever Bottersnike he waddled into the Bush trying to look bold, still muttering: 'Nincombotters, that's what they are, absolute Poopsnikes.'

*   *   *

Soon after Chank had gone the King of the Bottersnikes woke up. He had been asleep on and off for two weeks and now was tired of resting. He poked his head out of the window of his rusty car and roared: 'Snonk!'

The King said: 'Amuse me.'

The Bottersnikes blinked.

'Do something funny,' the King shouted. 'Make me laugh. Go on, make me laugh.'

Two young Bottersnikes tried to amuse the King by standing on their heads and waving their legs in the air — which, come to think of it, *is* rather a funny sight, but the King did not laugh.

29

'Idiots!' he growled, 'What's funny about standing on their heads? Now if they were to sit on 'em it might be quite amusing. Sit on 'em,' he added, 'Hard.'

Glob remarked that the funniest thing he could think of would be watching Chank trying to climb a tree, to get his roof down; and they told the King what had happened while he was asleep.

'All right,' said the King, 'We will go and watch.'

The other Bottersnikes did not like the idea of having to waddle so far but the King, well rested from his fortnight's sleep, was ready for a little exercise, especially as the others would have to carry him.

'If he's not funny,' the King said, 'We'll sit on his head.'
They took their jam tins with them, just in case.

★　★　★

The Gumbles had nearly forgotten the Bottersnikes because they are always too busy having fun to think of the nastier things. Besides, it was Spring and just now they were going to help a willie wagtail build her nest. But the mother wagtail was being very difficult about it, very choosey.

'First of all I must have the right place,' she said, 'Where the crows can't see it and the snakes can't climb.'

There was something wrong with all the cosy nesting places the Gumbles found for her.

'What about that thing up there?' Happigumble said at last. 'It looks like an old straw hat caught in the tree.'

'It might do,' Wagtail said doubtfully, 'But it's rather high up. What would happen if the babies fell out before they could fly?'

'We'll put it lower down for you,' the Gumbles said. They were tired of Wagtail's fuss and glad of an excuse to go and

climb something. At the foot of the tree, though, they got a fright that nearly made them jump out of their Gumbleskins. They saw a fat Bottersnike, flat on his back and snoring.

It was Chank, of course, come for his roof. He was too fat to climb the tree and his long waddle had tired him out.

All the Gumbles together need not be afraid of one Bottersnike, especially when he is sound asleep; so they hid his jam tin in a bush, to be on the safe side, pulled faces at him and climbed up the inside of the tree because it was a hollow one. There was a sort of window high up where a branch had broken off, and they climbed through that and got the hat and threw it down — it landed on Chank's head where it belonged.

Now they found it harder to get down. They were going to make themselves into a Gumblerope and climb down that when a Tink came from Tinkingumble.

'I've got a better way,' he said, peering from the window at the top of the trunk, 'We can jump.'

'O, no! It's too high!'

'On to Chank's tummy,' he said. 'Watch!'

He stood on the edge of the tree window, closed his eyes and went down with a Wheee! and a Berlumf! as he landed on Chank. He bounced off the great, fat stomach into the leaves beneath the tree, not hurt a bit.

The others were not slow to follow. Down they came one after the other with a Wheee Berlumf! Wheee Berlumf! on to Chank — it was like bouncing on a springy mattress, though more fun because more dangerous.

'That was good!' the Gumbles cried, 'Let's do it again!' and they scrambled up the inside of the hollow trunk and came down Wheee Berlumf! with their eyes shut. Chank did not wake up as he was so tired, but all that berlumfing on his tummy gave him bad dreams: he was being crawled over by a caterpillar as big as a crocodile with hobnailed boots on each of its fifty feet. It was fortunate he wasn't Smiggles.

The Gumbles thought this was one of the best games they'd had since last Spring. While they were waiting for their turn to jump they tried to make up a Gumblesong about it, but they couldn't think of a rhyme for Berlumf.

Suddenly the noise changed to Wheee Blap! though they didn't know why; they thought it might be easier to find a rhyme for Blap, but by the time they found out why they were going Blap instead of Berlumf it was too late to be bothering about Gumblesongs.

The rest of the Bottersnikes had arrived, expecting to have a good laugh at Chank — but this was better, much better! They sneaked past the tree one at a time, each holding out his tin and catching the Gumbles before they bounced on Chank. Naturally, the noise of their falling changed to Blap.

Chank woke up just in time to catch little Willigumble, who was the last to jump. He couldn't find his jam tin and had to put him in his roof instead. Chank was very pleased to have his roof back though annoyed at not finding his jam tin, because it was the one with the wire handle. It was a good thing he did not find the tin as Wagtail had lined it with soft grass and laid an egg in it.

CHAPTER FOUR

The Rainmaker

The Bottersnikes threw the Gumbles in the air a few times so
that they could shout 'Got you!' and grab them, and pop
them in the jam tins again, and have the job done the right
and proper way; then they shouted 'Home now!' and began
the long waddle back to the rubbish heaps.

Bottersnikes do not often sing, which is a good thing as
their singing sounds like hacksaws cutting tin, but they sang
this time because they were so pleased to have the Gumbles
back.

'Come on, Gumble,
Into the trap,
Watch him tumble —
Wheee Blap!'

The Gumbles did not think it was a good song at all but the Bottersnikes laughed and laughed until you'd think they had dreadful colds and no hankies. Chank was the merriest of all, but he wouldn't have laughed so loudly if he had known what had happened in his roof.

Willigumble had fallen out through one of the ear holes.

He hid until he was sure the Bottersnikes had not seen him, then followed at a safe distance.

Chank didn't find out until they got back to the rubbish heaps at night time — then he flew into a red-eared rage! He stormed up and down shouting that it wasn't fair, he should have two Gumbles, not none, and anyway no one would have any Gumbles at all if it hadn't been for him being brave and clever; but no one took the slightest notice and the King roared: 'Snonk!'

The King said: 'Bottersnikes! Thanks to me being a re-markable King, we got the Gumbles back. I deserve a party. Fortunately it is my birthday the day after tomorrow.'

'Hoo, hoo, hoo!' the Bottersnikes yelled, 'The King's Party!'

The Gumbles sighed. They guessed how much extra nasty work there would be.

The King had a birthday four or five times a year, or oftener if he felt like it, and each birthday they had a big party that lasted about three days. This time they would have the Gumbles to do all the work.

The King went on: 'The Gumbles will make ready for my party tomorrow. If it is fine.'

'Oh, yes. If it is fine,' the others said. 'Let's go and see the Weathersnike.'

It is no use the Bottersnikes thinking of having a party if it is going to rain, of course, and when they want to know what the weather is going to be they go and see the Weathersnike. The Weathersnike is a very old and wrinkly Bottersnike who lives under an upturned bath and seldom leaves it. He is very fat and very important, and never gets his head sat on — perhaps because, unlike the rest, he has sharp little horns.

The Weathersnike has a dish outside his bathtub which he uses as a rain gauge to measure the rain that falls, and he has a shadow stick stuck in the ground and when he sees a shadow from it he knows the sun is shining. Then he has a chimney poked through the plug hole of his bath for the soot to fall down and a piece of seaweed hung up which goes limp and wet when it is going to rain; and he listens to frogs croaking and watches swallows flying low and ants building roofs to their nests and all the other signs that mean bad weather. When he is asked for a forecast he will potter importantly about his instruments, as he calls them, and say 'Hum!' and 'Well now,' but, truth to tell, what he really goes by is whether his corns hurt or not.

'Wake up, Weathersnike,' the Bottersnikes bawled, and they bumped and thumped and banged and danced on the bath tub until the Weathersnike crawled out, a bit red-eared at being disturbed in the middle of the night.

'Tell us if it's going to rain. It's the King's Party the day after tomorrow.' They had to shout loud as the Weathersnike is rather deaf.

'Ho, hum!' said the Weathersnike, 'King's Party, eh? Well now, let me see.' He pottered about his instruments and looked at his shadow stick. 'Aha! The sun's not shining,' he said importantly.

'Of course it's not shining,' the King snapped. 'It's the middle of the night.'

'Middle of what?' said the Weathersnike.

'The night,' roared the King.

'Well, it might,' the Weathersnike agreed, 'But then again it might not. You can't take chances with the weather.'

'How can the sun be shining if it's the middle of the night?' bawled the King.

'It's *not* shining,' said the Weathersnike, 'I've just told you that weren't you listening?'

'The sun's not shining *because* it's the middle of the night,' roared the King whose ears were lighting up like beacons.

'If it's the middle of the night how do you expect me to know if the sun's shining or not?' replied the Weathersnike

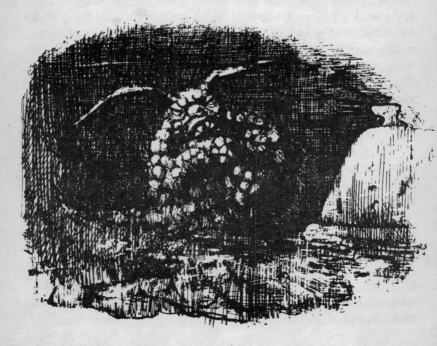

angrily. 'You're just wasting my time! Come back in the morning and I'll tell you then,' and he crawled under his bathtub.

'Idiot!' the King shouted — but he was too tired to argue with the weather expert any more. He staggered to his car and fell asleep. Soon they were all snoring as loud as steam trains.

When he heard the noise as loud as trains little Willigumble thought it safe to appear. He scrambled over the rubbish and found his friends flattened out in their jam tins. He went round to them all, Happigumble, Jolligumble, Merrigumble and the rest, but they were too tightly wodged in for Willi to get them out on his own. He just wasn't strong enough.

'Try and have a Tink, Tinkingumble,' he said. 'There must be some way of getting you out.' Tinkingumble tried and tried, but no Tink came.

'It's no good,' said the Tinker in a muffled voice, 'I must be squashed up too hard.'

'O, dear!' said Willi. Until now Tinkingumble had always managed some sort of a Tink when needed most, even if only a small one.

'With this King's Party coming up too!' Willi groaned, 'This is the worst jam we've ever been in,' He went from tin to tin trying to cheer people up, but he felt so sad himself that he was not much good at it.

'Stop trying to cheer us up, Willi,' Happigumble said, 'And mind you don't get caught yourself.'

Willigumble mooched around. 'I've got to think of something. I've got to,' he kept saying. But the job was too big for little Willi this time, it seemed.

Being hot and dusty after his long walk, he decided to take a bath. Near the Weathersnike's home he found a shallow dish that did not leak; this he filled with water, and hopped in. Good ideas sometimes come whilst bathing, even to people

who are not Tinkers. As he was splashing in his shallow dish a little thought came that seemed quite silly at first, but it grew and grew till it became bigger than Willi himself.

He jumped out of the bath and began the busiest night of his life.

First he scraped some soot from an old stove, wrapped it in a paper parcel and asked a bat to perch it on the Weathersnike's chimney. He threw water at the seaweed until it went wet and limp; he searched till he found a fork, and used it to dig up the shadow stick which he dragged away and hid. He went into the Bush, into all the damp places where there were frogs, and whispered something to each one.

'All right, Willigumble,' they croaked, 'We don't mind helping.'

After talking to the frogs he met Spiny Anteater, shuffling along looking for ants. 'The very person I wanted to see!' said Willi, and showed him a large ant heap outside the Weathersnike's bath tub.

Then he spent a long time looking for someone and, when he had found him, a long time talking.

At last he came back, chuckling all over with little Gumble-chuckles. 'There won't be any King's Party work for you tomorrow,' he told his squashed-up mates. 'The King won't be having a birthday. You see.' That was all he would say. Leaving the Gumbles rather bewildered, Willi climbed a tree and settled down comfortably to wait for morning.

Next day the sun rose into a cloudless sky. It promised to be a lovely day for a picnic, or for the Bottersnikes to have a Party, and the Gumbles groaned: 'Just our luck!' The sun was quite hot by the time the Bottersnikes woke. They yawned, stretched and remembered they had to go and see the Weathersnike.

'Wake up, Weathersnike,' they bawled, and banged and danced and bumped on the bath — down came the bag of soot that Willigumble's bat had perched on the chimney. The Weathersnike crawled out looking blacker than usual.

'Tut, bad sign,' he said, brushing off soot.

He looked at his piece of seaweed. It was limp and wet because, during the night, Willigumble had soaked it. 'Tut tut,' said the Weathersnike.

He looked at the ants who were climbing trees and building roofs to their nests and rushing madly about because, during the night, Spiny Anteater had frightened them so. 'Tut tut tut,' said the Weathersnike. 'Worse and worse!'

He looked for the shadow of his shadow stick and couldn't see it because the stick wasn't there and said: 'Tut tut tut tut!'

He looked at his rain gauge which was brimming with Willigumble's bathwater and said: 'Rained hard in the night. Tut tut tut tut tut!'

The King of the Bottersnikes was getting impatient. 'Don't stand there going like a motor bike — tell us if it's going to stay fine!'

'You can't take chances with the weather,' said the Weathersnike very wisely. 'The signs are so bad I shouldn't be surprised if it was raining already.'

The Bottersnikes looked anxiously at themselves to see if they were shrinking. There would have been a good old red-eared argument about it, but all the frogs within half a mile started croaking 'Arrk-oak, arrk-oak,' because, during the night, Willigumble had asked them to.

'That's another bad sign,' said the Weathersnike, 'Tut tut tut tut tut —'

Owl interrupted this line of tuts by looking out of his hollow tree — not because Willigumble had asked him to, only because he felt like it — and remarking: 'Too wet to whoo!' Or so it sounded.

'I know it is!' the Weathersnike shouted, 'Tut tut tut tut tut — ouch, my corns! Oh, my corns!' They had started shooting like anything, and that was because Yabby, the crayfish, had nipped his toes *hard* — and Yabby was the someone Willigumble had spent a long time talking to during the night.

'I've never known it more likely to rain in my whole fore-casting career. I'm going in before I shrink,' the Weathersnike declared, and he hobbled into his bath tub to nurse his painful feet.

The Bottersnikes, who were getting hot standing in the sun, didn't know what to think. Then one of the King's red hot ears sizzled as though a drop of rain had fallen on it. They heard it plainly — SSSSsssss!

'My birthday will be postponed until the weather im-proves,' announced the King hastily. He retired to his palace as fast as he could waddle.

Little Willigumble (who had squeezed the drop of rain from a piece of wet moss) laughed until he nearly fell out of the tree.

CHAPTER FIVE

Spring in the Air

'The King's Party is going to be put off until it stops raining,' Willigumble whispered to Happigumble and the others nearby, 'So there won't be any nasty work for you for a bit. Now we've got to find a way of getting you out of the jam tins. I'll go and see if Tinkingumble's managed to have a Tink yet — he's sure to think of something.'

He scurried across to Tinkingumble's tin, taking care the Bottersnikes did not see him. This was not difficult. They were all under cover so as not to get wet in the sun. The King was in his car, Chank was wearing his roof, the Weathersnike was under his bath tub as usual and the rest were skulking beneath their pots and pans, bits of iron, mattresses, kettles, watering cans and buckets, waiting for the rain that never came.

'No,' said Tinkingumble sadly, 'I haven't had a Tink, and I've tried and tried. D'you know what, Willigumble? I think I've lost my Tink!'

'Perhaps you dropped it somewhere,' Willigumble suggested. 'I'll go and hunt for it. What does it look like?'

Neither knew for certain. They imagined it would be a small bag with a bell that rang as each good idea popped out.

'I'll get the bees to help me look,' said Willi, trying to sound cheerful, 'They go everywhere.'

Willigumble went off. It was a lovely spring day with a blue sky and a breeze that blew in playful puffs, just enough to keep the leaves from dozing. Down below, flowers were warming themselves in the sun, the bitter peas, red spiders and coral heath in the damp places; bees were busy looking for pollen and birds flying for the fun of it. Lower still, right on the warm earth, thousands of ants, beetles and spiders were on the move, each one busy doing what it should do on a fine spring morning.

It is good to be friendly with these little people. Willigumble was, and very soon he had an army of ants and bees, birds, cicadas, frogs and spiders helping him by keeping an eye open as they went about their work, but none of them saw anything that looked like the lost Tink.

'Whew! The Bush is a big place,' said Willigumble, after he had been searching for a long time without success, 'And we're not even sure what the Tink looks like. I'd better have a rest and a think.' He sat on an old spring mattress in the rubbish, far enough from the Bottersnikes to be safe. The cover was quite rotten and he fell in amongst the springs and the things that happen in old mattresses, but it did not matter. Wiligumble settled in the coil of a spring and bounced lightly to help him think things over.

'Now I'm out,' he thought, 'And the rest are in — tins, that is. They can't get out and I'm not strong enough to pull them out. Tinkingumble's lost his Tink and it can't be found, and if they don't escape soon, by Tink or by think, there'll be all that horrible work to do for the King's Party. This is serious. Very serious.'

There came a loud laugh from a branch above his head. Hahahahahohohohohaha!' Kookaburra, of course.

'Lovely day,' remarked the bird to Willigumble. 'What are you doing down there?'

'I'm thinking how serious it is.'

'Ar, it doesn't do to think,' said Kookaburra. 'Bad for the brain. That's the trouble with you ground creatures. Too much thinking, not enough flying. Look at those Bottersnikes now — what do they *think* they're doing, cooped up in their pots and pans on a lovely day like this?'

'They think it's going to rain,' said Willigumble.

'Hahahahahohoho! Rain? On a day like this? This is the sort of day that makes you glad to be a bird,' Kookaburra said, 'Why, it's spring in the air today!'

'What's that?' said Willigumble, bouncing higher.

'What's the matter with you? I said spring's in the air. Can't you feel it?'

'Grasshoppers!' shouted Willigumble. 'Spring. In the air. I believe you're right! Help me, please, Kookaburra, with your strong beak,' and he did a very strange thing for a Gumble. He began pulling the old mattress to bits.

'Everybody's mad!' said Kookaburra.

With the help of the astonished bird Willigumble had stripped the rotting cover from the mattress and laid bare the springs when they heard shouting and snuffle-nose noises from the Bottersnikes, and saw smoke rising.

'Have they started a bushfire?' Willigumble asked anxiously.

It wasn't a bushfire. It was Chank's roof. Chank had got angry waiting for the rain that didn't rain and his straw hat had caught alight from his red hot ears.

Chank was extremely angry when he saw that his beautiful roof was smouldering, and the angrier he became the hotter the fire flared. The other Bottersnikes stood giving good advice but they did not do anything to put the fire out.

'It must be cosy in there with a nice fire,' Snorg said.

'But you should have a chimney to let the smoke out,' said Glob.

'Keep still, Chank, while we cook a bit of toast,' and they snuffled in high glee.

Slightly overheated now, Chank started running about madly. He could not see where he was going — how those fat

Bottersnikes hopped when Chank and his blazing top-knot came blundering among them. This part, they thought, was not so funny, and the King was not at all amused because Chank was coming near his car.

'What's that idiot doing running around on fire?' he roared. 'Sit on his head!'

The Bottersnikes blinked at this because Chank's head was obviously too hot to sit on, but the King was angry and not to be put off.

'But King, we can't —' they said.

'Yes you can,' he bawled, 'If he's got a head it can be sat on, so sit on it, hard, and don't argue.'

'We'll get burned!'

'I don't care,' the King screamed. 'If somebody doesn't sit on his head in less than no time I won't have a birthday when it stops raining, and there'll be no King's Party.'

This would never do. The Bottersnikes hurried to their jam tins and let the Gumbles go with orders to put the fire out quick smart so that Chank could have his head sat on. The Gumbles were glad to be out of the tins at last and made a great show as firefighters.

First they tripped Chank up by thrusting a stick between his legs. The straw hat had nearly burned away by now but somehow — no one quite knew how — the fire spread alarmingly. A patch of dry bladey grass exploded into flames. Billows of vile smoke went up from an old bag that caught alight. Gumbles, rushing about with hoses, tackled the job manfully. But seemed to be making the fire worse. The hoses would keep getting wound round the Bottersnikes' legs. Many a tail was scorched, accidentally. And the noise! There was a wailing from the roofless Chank and yelping from the owners of scorched tails, while the fire was roaring and the King was roaring and smoke made everyone cough. Altogether there was far more smoke, sparks, shouting and confusion than when the Gumbles were safely in their jam tins.

At last the King made his voice heard above the uproar: "Them Gumbles ain't doing any good! Put 'em in their jam tins and squash 'em down hard!' So the Bottersnikes grabbed the Gumble firemen and groped through the smoke for the tins. They popped them in and squashed them down most savagely but instead of flattening out like lumps of dough as they were supposed to, the Gumbles came shooting out of their tins as if on springs. This was not so surprising. They were on springs. Willigumble and Kookaburra had put a mattress spring in each tin while everyone was busy with the fire.

The Gumbles held on to the springs with their toes and went zoinng! zoinng! over the heads of the startled Bottersnikes like rubber Kangaroos. The Bottersnikes were too amazed to do anything except rub their smoke-filled eyes and watch the Gumbles zoinnging down the hill into the Bush.

Willigumble was bouncing along on a spring of his own.

'Sorry we can't —' zoinng! — 'stay for the King's Party —' zoinng! — he shouted, 'But we have to —' zoinng! — 'go now. Spring's in the air, you know!' and he bounced after the others as fast as he could zoinng.

CHAPTER SIX

Smiggles Does the Right Thing

No one can remember a time when the Bottersnikes were as angry as they were this time, when they saw the Gumbles springing away to the Bush on their springs. They hopped in circles out of sheer rage and tripped over each others' tails, and their ears became like crimson bottlebrushes though not as pretty. After a time they forgot what they were supposed to be angry about but went on hopping just the same until the King yelled 'Snonk!' most fiercely.

He kept them snonking a long time so that he could have some peace to tickle his tummy with the end of his tail and at last the King said: 'We will have to fetch them back.'

'Oh, clever,' the Bottersnikes cried, 'Then we'll be able to have the Party.'

'Jam tins ready,' roared the King, 'Quick waddle!' Off they went, puffing and wheezing and determined to recapture their servants. It was easy to see which way they had gone. The springs had left clear zoinng marks on the ground and the Bottersnikes could follow by tracking. Some fell asleep on the way but the rest followed the tracks to the creek, where the zoinng marks stopped at the water's edge. There were no boats, no bridges, no Gumbles.

The Bottersnikes glared at the water, hit it with sticks and growled: 'Beastly stuff! How are we going to track them over that?'

There was no need. The Gumbles had sprung to a little island in the creek where they were safe with water all around. They had put their springs in a bin marked Please Be Tidy and now were standing on the shore, laughing.

'Beautiful day,' they called cheerily across the water. 'Are you going to have the King's Party today?'

'How did you get over there?' screamed the Bottersnikes, 'Come back the same way, and jump to it!'

'We can't,' they said, 'Our springs have run down. We're stranded!' It made the Gumbles giggly, watching the Bottersnikes' ears go red. They chanted 'Save us, save us, won't you come and save us?' to make them redder still, and when the ears were glowing with fury they cheekily waved goodbye and went to find some Gumbletricks to get up to. Though only a small island there was enough on it to keep them happy — all except Tinkingumble, who was still a bit sad at losing his Tink.

The King of the Bottersnikes made two of his band get down on their hands and knees to make a sort of throne for him, and there he sat majestically tickling his tummy with the end of his tail. After two minutes of this the King said: 'We want a bridge.'

'Clever, as usual,' admired the others — still, there were no bridges lying about, no planks, no dead branches, nothing to help them over the creek.

'We could try Smiggles again,' someone suggested.

'Idiot!' the King snorted. But he was unable to think of anything better, so he called Smiggles and ordered: 'Go to sleep, Smiggles, and dream a bridge. A strong one.' Smiggles was delighted at the chance of a nap and went to sleep at once, before falling to the ground with a thud.

'Smiggles is all very well,' said Globb, 'But he'll probably dream something quite wrong. He'll probably dream a thunderstorm.'

'Or a scrubbing brush,' added Snorg.

'Or a water melon.'

'Or a garbage collector.'

'All right then, you cleversnikes,' the King roared, 'Build another bridge yourselves! Go on, build one!'

'What of?' they asked.

'Idiots!' the King raged, 'I've told you what to do, now all you got to do is do it. Have a bridge built by the time I —' He fell asleep before he could say 'wake-up.'

Chank thought that this was his chance, while the King was asleep, to show the others how clever he really was. He had been looking at a tall stringybark tree close to the creek; one branch leaned over the water.

'It's quite easy to anyone a bit clever,' he said. 'What we have to do is saw off that branch. It would fall across the creek and make a beaut bridge. All you really want is brains.'

'The only other thing we really want,' said Glob, 'Is a saw.'

There was an old saw on the rubbish heaps as a matter of fact but no one wanted to waddle all the way back to get it. Instead they looked until they saw a see-saw; they broke it in halves, threw the see half away and used the saw to fell the branch. It was hard work though. Four Bottersnikes had to stand on each others' heads to reach the branch while the top one, Chank, did the sawing.

It was a hot and bothering business, but at last the branch came down just as Chank had intended . . . and Smiggles woke up.

'I've done it!' he shouted proudly, 'I've dreamed a bridge. Look!'

Smiggles had done the right thing. There was a beautiful timber bridge, big enough to drive a car over, with white rails and notices at each end that said No Fishing Allowed, but it was on the *other* side of the island; as the Bottersnikes blinked and looked they saw the last of the Gumbles scampering over it, waving cheekily and escaping to the Bush.

The Bottersnikes gave chase. They had to cross Chank's bridge first, run over the island, then cross Smiggles' bridge, and by then the Gumbles were safely hidden in ferns and under roots where the Bottersnikes could never find them, though they hunted till they were very tired.

They called Smiggles all the names they could think of for dreaming his bridge on the wrong side of the island. Smiggles replied that he'd been told to dream a bridge and he'd dreamed one, and it was a beauty, and if people would stop criticizing the world would be a better place. There was going to be a first rate red-eared shouting match about this when they saw the notices which said No Fishing Allowed. Bottersnikes cannot resist doing something that is not allowed. They growled: 'Oho, Smiggles, just you wait till the King wakes up!' and started to fish from the bridge at once. When the King did wake he found them dangling lines of creeper in the water, with hooks made from wire pulled from their own wiry tails.

The King looked at Chank's bridge and snorted, then he looked at Smiggles' bridge and said: 'Well dreamed, Smiggles, my boy. A very sound bridge,' and he patted him on the head. 'Now, where are the Gumbles?' went on the King. 'Jam tins ready. Quick waddle home for my birthday.'

This was awkward. The Bottersnikes blinked and got ready to have their heads sat on. Smiggles, who did not often get patted on the head, saved the day for them with a bright little lie: 'The Gumbles jumped in the water before I finished dreaming. So we're fishing for 'em. There's no fishing allowed,' he added proudly.

The King was not as angry as they had feared. Only the tips of his ears went red. He muttered: 'Chuk chuk chuk! Well, give me a fishing line.'

So they all sat and fished from the bridge, and very pleasant it was, only it is doubtful if they caught any fish. Cetainly they did not catch any Gumbles, who were watching the fishersnikes from their hiding places under roots and ferns and sniggering very quietly.

It was quiet and peaceful with the water gurgling under the bridge, and from time to time the King patted Smiggles' head and told him he was a good 'snike and could sit next to him at the Party. It made Chank jealous. Smiggles, however, was more accustomed to having his head sat on than patted. A dreamy look came into his eyes and his patted head began to nod.

Chank suddenly screamed: 'Wake up, Smiggles!'

It was nearly in time — not quite. Smiggles half went to sleep and half his dream bridge vanished. The Bottersnikes who had been sitting on the vanished half fell straight into the creek and the King, who had been in the middle, see-sawed for a long second — time enough to bellow: 'Sit on that idiot's —' before falling into the water with a king-sized splash.

CHAPTER SEVEN

'Clunk!'

Fortunately for the Bottersnikes it was a good drying day and those that had fallen in the water were soon dry after they had been hanging up by their tails for a bit. Smiggles had not fallen in. His head had been sat on most severely and now the King was making him sit on what was left of his dream bridge. This was awkward for Smiggles because he was tired and badly wanted forty winks, but he knew what would happen if he took them.

The other Bottersnikes sat in red-eared circle on the island trying to think of another Gumbletrap. As for the Gumbles themselves, they had tiptoed away and were playing hide and seek with some lizards.

'Now what I think,' said Chank importantly, 'Is this. I think it's the one what goes 'Tink' what causes all the bother. That's what I think.' (He was not to know, of course, that Tinkingumble had lost his Tink.)

'It's a pity you don't tink instead of thinking so much,' said Glob in his nasty way. 'It'd be much more useful.'

'Nincomsnike!' shouted Chank angrily — and would have said much more but the King roared 'Snonk!' very loudly.

The King said: 'Can any Bottersnike go tink?'

They all tried, and went tink in their fat growly voices, but none of them sounded a bit like Tinkingumble and no good ideas came. In fact it sounded more like a lot of crows trying to sing Pop Goes the Weasel and it made the King's ears ache.

'Idiots!' he shouted. 'Tink! — I mean Snonk! That tinking Gumble don't say tink. He just goes tink like as if the noise came from inside.'

'Like hitting the edge of a glass with a spoon,' said Chank.

'Like hitting you on the head with a lump of wood,' roared the King, who was tired of Chank's being clever all the time. He tried it to see. Chank's head was so thick and hard that when whacked with a stick it just went Clack!

'No good at all,' roared the King happily.

'Just goes Clack! Hark at it! Clack!

Clack! Clack!' The King was enjoying himself no end. He whacked as many Bottersnikes as he could catch on the head to see if any would go tink, but their heads were so thick and hard they all sounded the same as Chank's.

'Not a tink in the whole darned lot of you,' the King growled, brandishing his stick. 'I never heard a more clack-headed lot of Bottersnikes in my life.'

'Try hitting yourself on the head, then,' suggested Smiggles cheekily. The King could not reach him where he was sitting on the bridge.

'No one will ever know what my head sounds like,' the King bawled. 'Kings don't get whacked on the head. That's why they're Kings. Anyway you go to sleep, Smiggles. Go on. Go to sleep.'

Smiggles didn't go to sleep — he dared not — though he closed his eyes a moment to make the King stop yelling at him. Maybe it was through Smiggles closing his eyes, maybe white ants had been eating the wood — whatever the cause, one of the No Fishing notices just then began to topple over. The King did not see it falling, and it whacked him on the head so hard that it drove him in the ground up to his waist. But the interesting thing was that the royal head did not go Clack like the others; it made a good, hollow, satisfying Clunk! — which proves that Kings' heads are different.

The No Fishing notice disappeared, and the King looked surprised to find himself waist deep in the earth. 'Come and get me out of this bog,' he said. 'I've just had an idea for the best Gumbletrap of all.' He seemed not to have felt the whack

63

on his head a bit. He called the others into a ring around him and talked, and as he talked the circle of red-hot ears gradually stopped glowing and became an ordinary dirty black.

'. . . something like a bird with a broken wing,' the King was saying, 'Crying piteously for help, and the Gumbles, being soft-hearted things, will come along to see what the cries are about, and we'll jump out of the bushes and grab 'em —'

'And shout "Got You"!'

'And pop 'em into jam tins —'

'And quick waddle home for the King's Party! Hoo, hoo, hoo! That's the best Gumbletrap of all!' and the Bottersnikes leaped around as gleefully as if they had caught the Gumbles already.

'Only thing,' said Glob, stopping a leap in mid-air and falling to the ground with a thud, 'What are we going to do for a bird with a broken wing?'

'Aha!' the King said, 'That is the cleverest part of my clever idea. Chank!'

Chank jumped a foot out of fright and turned pale.

'Be a bird with a broken wing,' ordered the King. 'Go on. Be one!'

Chank protested that though he was clever at most things, being a bird with a broken wing was not one of the things he was particularly clever at and that he could be much cleverer being clever at something else. No one listened.

So he got down on the ground and rolled about, feebly flapping one arm, and called out in a piteous fat growly voice: 'Help help! I'm a poor little boidie wiv a broken wing, how's that?'

He didn't look at all like a bird, only like a fat Bottersnike rolling on the ground.

'That's not nearly clever enough,' the King snorted, and he tickled his tummy a bit. At last he said: 'He's too big. Shrink him.'

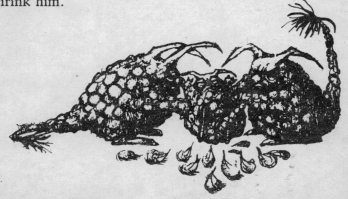

Taking no notice of Chank's howls they dipped him carefully in the creek until he was about as big as a pigeon. They put him on the bank opposite the island and tucked his wiry tail in so it wouldn't show; a few feathers scattered about helped to make it look real, then, with the Gumbletrap set, they hid themselves securely in the Bush.

The Gumbles were hiding too, from the lizards. It was the lizards' turn to seek.

'No peeping now!' they shouted, for these lizards were tricky that way — they had no eyelids to close.

The Gumbles ducked into long grass and hurried towards the creek. Not a 'snike to be seen! On what was left of Smiggles' bridge they smartly made themselves into a Gumblerope, which is a bit like a string of sausages; one end of the Gumblerope tied itself in a half-hitch around a bridge rail, the other threw itself over the water and landed on the island. The half-hitch undid itself and the other end hauled in until the whole Gumblerope was safely over the water. It was very pretty to watch.

Then they saw Chank.

'Careful!' they said to each other, 'It's a Bottersnike.'

'I'm not a Bottersnike!' said Chank angrily, 'I'm a poor little boidie wiv a broken wing. Help help!' he added.

The Gumbles could see perfectly well that he was a Bottersnike and not a bird, but they couldn't resist having a bit of fun with a chance like this. 'Poor little birdie,' they called, 'How did you break your wing?'

'Fell outa that tree, I did,' said Chank. Came down plop when they sawed that branch off to make a bridge. Took me by surprise, see?'

'Ah!' said Happigumble with a wink, 'That was a clever idea, to make a bridge like that.'

Chank sat up and beamed. 'It was clever, wasn't it? That was my idea. I'm the cleverest Bottersnike of the lot and I ought to be the —'

'You just said you weren't a Bottersnike,' said Jolligumble. 'What sort of a bird are you?'

'You heard wrong,' said Chank quickly. 'I said, er, cuckooshrike.' (There's brains for you, he thought.)

'Sing us a song, Cuckoo-shrike!' the Gumbles begged.

'Twee twee-twee!' growled Chank.

'It was the fall he had,' the Gumbles sniggered, 'Must have broken his voice as well, poor bird.' They made him fearfully mixed then by asking questions about mother Cuckoo-shrike's nest and her eggs, for Gumbles know all about these things; Chank said they were very fond of eggs and and had them hard boiled mostly. The Gumbles began to go giggly, which turned the Cuckoo-shrike's ears bright scarlet.

'Stop asking silly questions,' he shouted. 'Come over and help me with my broken wing.'

'Suppose we hang you up by your tail,' Jolligumble suggested, 'And you can sing us another song while you're drying out.'

'If you promise the others won't grab us,' Happigumble had sense enough to add.

Quick and crafty, Chank said: 'Grab you? Oh no! They've all gone home. To have the King's Party.'

Those silly Gumbles, who were quite giggly, believed him. They trooped over the sawn-off branch and with a one-two-three altogether pull they hoisted the shrunk Chank by his tail into a banksia bush where he would catch the wind.

'Now sing us another song,' they said.

'Chippy chippy tweet tweet,' sang Chank.

Once again, and once too often, the Gumbles went giggly. Rolling about quite hopelessly, quite helplessly, they suddenly found themselves surrounded by a ring of green and wrinkled faces with long red ears, upward slanted eyes, noses like coal scuttles and little toadstools —

'Got You!' shouted the Bottersnikes, and they grabbed those little giggling Gumbles and popped them into jam tins.

CHAPTER EIGHT

The King's Party

Bottersnikes eat pictures of food in papers and magazines. There are plenty of these in rubbish heaps — that's partly why they are so fat. Also they eat the stuffing out of mattresses. This they like fried. For sweets they are fond of rusty nails, though their favourites are milk bottle tops, which they chew like chewing gum. They will eat earwigs and cardboard too, but only if they are hungry.

So the Gumbles had to go through all the rubbishy papers carefully cutting out the food pictures. They had to search the junk heaps from end to end for bottle tops and rusty nails and, worst of all, they had to carry in the stuffing from four mattresses and pile it ready for frying. The Bottersnikes yelled at them all day long.

By evening everything was nearly ready. The Gumbles had built a large table from sheets of iron propped on bricks, and a stone fireplace too, to do the cooking on.

From the roof of his palace the King bawled: 'Light the
fire and fry the stuffing!'

Firelighting was the one job the Bottersnikes did themselves. As no one happened to be angry at the time, they
grabbed a snoozing 'snike, thrust his head into the fireplace
and kicked him and twisted his tail until he was thoroughly
enraged. The kindling quickly caught from his red hot ears
and the fire blazed in no time.

In great excitement, Smiggles woke from a little nap he
happened to be taking. 'Look what I done!' he shouted, 'Look
what I gone and dreamed!'

'You wasn't ordered to dream anything, Smiggles,' the
King roared. 'Sit on his head!'

'But it's tomato soup!' Smiggles protested. It was too, a
large tureen of it, rich, red and steaming, fresh from the

depths of Smig's sleep. 'I dreamed it special,' he added craft-ily, 'As a birthday present.'

The King could not be angry. Everyone loves tomato soup. Yet care had to be taken lest the present vanished before it could be used; so Smiggles was hung up by his tail to stop him going to sleep. From time to time he was given a kick to make certain of his wakefulness, then a pat on the head to show there were no hard feelings.

Quite pleased with the gift of soup, the King announced, loudly: 'I will receive the rest of my birthday presents.'

The Bottersnikes blinked.

'Now,' the King said. And sat there waiting.

Once more the tired Gumbles had to comb the rubbish heaps, with the Bottersnikes waddling behind, this time for suitable presents for the King. His Majesty received a whistle, a water pistol, a mousetrap and a quantity of fruit, mostly rotten — the best that could be found at short notice.

Presently the King stood atop his car and blew a shrill blast on his new whistle. In the grand manner, the King said: 'Bottersnikes! I declare my birthday party open!' He took a flying leap from the roof of his palace and landed on the table, which tipped under his weight. Most of the party food slid his way and he grabbed all he could and sat on it. The others rushed in from the sidelines and yelled and fought for what was left — the idea being to grab all that could be grabbed and sit on it, then to try to steal from someone else's grabbing without getting caught.

With nothing left to grab, they pounded the iron table with their spoons, scratched their backs with their forks and shouted at each other in a 'snike-like way.

'My pile's bigger'n Glob's!' crowed Chank.

'But I got more stuffin'!' shouted Glob, and to prove it he hurled his table knife. His aim was bad and the knife stuck quivering in the Weathersnike's tummy. The weather expert folded his umbrella (he had brought it with him because, he

71

said, you can't take chances at a Party) and coshed Chank on the head, whereupon Chank groped under the table for a dead fish he'd hidden there and slapped Snorg in the face with it twice. So the Party got going.

All this time Smiggles was howling to be let down so that he could join in. With a shrill whistle blast the King announced that the soup would be served.

He served it in his water pistol. Dangerous jets of tomato soup shot everywhere. No one but the Weathersnike had an umbrella. The Bottersnikes found the safest place was under the table with their Gumbles held in front of them, rolled thin.

When all the soup had been served, or spilled, and Smiggles released, the King thought the Party needed livening up. Most of the Bottersnikes under the table were asleep. So the King started throwing things. The rest of his presents, the rotten fruit, were excellent for livening up the Party. Against a water pistol the Bottersnikes were helpless, but when the King threw rotten fruit they scraped it up and threw it back. The Party went fast and very furious. When the fruit became squashed to pulp they threw Gumbles instead — Gumbles could be thrown again and again.

Quite soon the King became tired of throwing the Party — he was being hit too often. Blowing a fierce blast on his whistle he yelled: 'Half time!'

Smiggles, who was very sore at missing so much of the fun, especially about the tail, took no notice. He hurled his last Gumble — it happened to be Tinkingumble — and scored a direct hit on the King's nose. This made Smiggles feel much better; less fortunately, it made the King swallow his whistle. It went on whistling inside him each time he took a deep breath.

The King was exceedingly angry. His ears glowed, his tummy whistled. He unwrapped Tinkingumble from his nose and rolled him in a tight ball to throw back. As he was about to throw a loud Tink sounded, clear as the call of a bellbird.

'Hooray!' shouted Tinkingumble, 'It wasn't lost after all. It only got stuck.'

'Quiet!' yelled the King. 'Feep!' went his tummy.

Tinkingumble couldn't help it. The King was squeezing very hard and it made him tink madly, like a cash register in Woolworths — every one a good idea.

'That's the one what causes all the bother,' said Chank airily.

73

'Cleversnike!' the King snarled, and threw Tinkingumble at him. The Tinker bounced and rolled under a bush, where he sat down to sort out at the good ideas that had come unstuck.

'Ar, it don't matter,' said Glob, helping himself to Chank's bottle tops, 'Clunks are better'n Tinks any day.'

Before this could be proved the King said: 'I will make a speech. Then we'll have a sleep. Then we'll throw some more Party. Grab them Gumbles and pop 'em in the jam tins.'

During the throwing the jam tins had been scattered far and wide, so to save themselves bother the Bottersnikes squashed the Gumbles together in one big mass in the empty soup tureen, saying they'd sort 'em out in the morning. This was worse for the Gumbles than jam tinning because those beneath could hardly breathe, but there was no help for it and there they had to stay while the King made his birthday speech.

The speech was long and dull. At first the Bottersnikes sat on the table and listened, pounding with their spoons at the important places, then one by one they dozed off and at last the King put himself to sleep with is own speech. Only Smiggles was awake — he had been hung up again to prevent the disappearance of the soup tureen. Old Smig wasn't having much of a party yet, but there was still two and a half days to go.

The Gumbles knew this too. Inside the soup tureen they were struggling and wriggling to escape, and they had found that they were not stuck to the bottom of the tureen as it was still slippery with thick red soup; but they were stuck fast to each other because the Bottersnikes had jammed them in so tightly.

'If we could only get unstuck from each other,' they thought, 'We'd be free!'

Push and wriggle as they might, they could not pull themselves apart. What they did manage to do was make themselves into one big Gumble — a clumsy creature, but it could walk and move its arms and waggle its huge head, and it could talk in a deep boomy voice . . . it was a Giant Gumble! little Willi was stuck on behind, like a tail. He wagged.

A bit soupy round the edges, the Giant Gumble stepped out of the tureen and loosened up, like a genie just out of a bottle.

'Yikes!' yelled Smiggles, who could not remember having dreamed a monster.

The Giant lifted Smiggles down, finding he could do it easily, and when the Giant found how strong he was he laughed 'Ho ho ho!' in his deep boomy voice. He put Smiggles in the soup tureen and slapped a lid on; from there, for the dreamer, sleep would be the only escape.

The Giant Gumble lumbered around, followed by his own huge shadow — for it was night now and the moon was up — and when the Giant saw how big his shadow was he laughed 'Ho ho ho!' in his booming giant's voice. He looked at the snoring 'snikes and knew that he need not be afraid.

'I am too big,' said that Giant, 'For a jam tin.'

Rattling about in the Giant's head was a bright idea that might once have been a Tink. With a long piece of rope he joined the Bottersnikes together — knotted it tightly around each tail a bit above the tassel, and the two ends of the rope he joined on the tail of the King.

'This Party,' said the Giant, 'Needs livening up.'

He overturned the table, Bottersnikes and all. They woke, hopping mad immediately. Someone's head needed sitting on, that was plain; up they got to see whose head it would be.

'Sit on it,' yelled the furious King, 'Till the middle of next week.'

'Foo!' said the Giant. The King fell over in astonishment. No one had said Foo! to him in his whole reign.

The Giant clambered to the roof of the King's palace and stood there right against the moon. He looked huge. Much too big to do as he was told.

'Waow!' yelled the Bottersnikes.

The King was not so easily scared. 'It's only Smiggles. He's been dreaming again,' he roared.

'No I ain't,' came a muffled voice from the soup tureen, 'I didn't have nothin' to do with it.'

Now the tureen was talking! — or so it seemed to the frightened 'snikes. One or two scaredy-cats tried to run away, but could not get far because of the rope around their tails. 'Lemme go!' they yelled, 'Stop pulling my tail!' 'Feep fee-eep!' went the King's tummy — the royal tail was being pulled too. Slowly at first, the Bottersnikes of the King's band, and the King too, began to go round in a circle, some trying to run away, some trying to stop their tails being pulled off — round they went, faster, faster, whirling, glowing, sparks shooting from their red hot ears, like a magnificent catherine wheel fit for a giant to watch; and once it was spinning nothing in the world could stop it . . . until the rope snapped. The catherine wheel burst into glowing stars then, and the Giant clapped his hands.

That was the end of the Party. He slid off the car and strode away to the Bush, still filling the moonlit night with the boom of his Ho ho ho! The Giant shook and rocked with laughter. The Giant shook himself to pieces.

Ordinary Gumbles came tumbling out of his arms and legs, his head and his tummy, and soon the Giant was lying in little Gumblebits and pieces on the ground. Very pleased to be their ordinary selves again, the bits and pieces scampered off to find some games to play in moonshine.

'No more Parties! No more jam tins!' they told each other, still giggling rather, 'And we'll never let ourselves get caught again — we'll never be so silly!'

They weren't quite right about that. Bottersnikes are always having Parties, and the trouble with Gumbles is that when they go giggly they are silly enough for anything.

★   ★   ★

Make sure that you cut all the food pictures out of papers and magazines before you throw them in the Bush, by the way. . . And be careful to remove the bottoms from your empty jam tins too — or better still, don't throw tins and papers into the Bush at all.